Night in Shining Armour

Manali Desai

Ukiyoto Publishing

All global publishing rights are held by

Ukiyoto Publishing

Published in 2024

Content Copyright © Manali Desai

ISBN 9789364942393

All rights reserved.

No part of this publication may be reproduced, transmitted, or stored in a retrieval system, in any form by any means, electronic, mechanical, photocopying, recording or otherwise, without the prior permission of the publisher.

The moral rights of the author have been asserted.

This book is sold subject to the condition that it shall not by way of trade or otherwise, be lent, resold, hired out or otherwise circulated, without the publisher's prior consent, in any form of binding or cover other than that in which it is published.

www.ukiyoto.com

Dedication

Dear Husband,
Let's say *I love you more than there are stars in the sky*
Let's say *You're my sun and stars*
But what's the point when
You won't say in return *I love you to the moon and back*
You won't say in return *You're the moon of my life*

P.S:
Me: 8
You: 1, 1.5, or is it 2?
Whatever. You're the math wizard. Do this at least
(8 = number of books written by Manali.
1/1.5/2 = number of those books read by the husband)

Contents

Facets	1
Unrequited Love	3
Friendship Goals	4
Scars to My Beautiful	5
Shall We Count Stars Together?	7
Avoiding the Crowd	8
Nightly Interlude	10
The Brightest Star	11
Quietude	12
Owl	13
Meteor	14
Jasmine	15
Ghost	16
Heaven and Earth	17
Readalong	18
Midas Touch	19
Paparazzi	20
At the End of the Day	21
Secured	22
Community	23
Lapping it Up	24
The Light at the End of the Tunnel	25
Cry Wolf	26
Not Alone	27
Pursuits	**28**
Routine	29
An Insomniac's Plight	30

Bonfire	31
Taken for a Ride	33
Dream or Goal?	34
Burning the Effigy	35
Fireworks	36
Zapper	37
Signs	38
Xanax	39
a(W)ake	40
Un(V)eil	41
Union	42
Tenting	43
Stargazing	45
Rooftop	46
Pajamas	47
Nightclub	48
Lovemaking	49
Call it A Night	50
Karaoke	51
Insomnia	52
Hunger	53
Do it All Tonight	54
Ouija	56
Burning the Midnight Oil	57
Preparing for the Morrow	58
Let's Make Tonight Special	59
A Dark Winter Night	60
The Force	62
For A Spin	64
Did That Happen	66

NiSA Playlist	67
Other Books by This Author	71
About the Author	**78**

Facets

Unrequited Love

Best paired with:
Chaand Bhi Koi Deewaana Hai (Apna Ghar Apni Kahaani, 1968)

Making the night bright,
With your whiteness.
Making the sky beautiful,
With your brightness.
Making the dark less gloomy,
With your glow.
Making the stars shine brighter,
With your company.
Making beauty less perfect,
With your many spots.

Oh! Inspiration of many songs and poems,
Oh! Beloved of the lovers and loners,
Do you also crave someone's love?
Why then do you show up just a little sometimes,
And sometimes all at once,
And sometimes not at all?

Maybe you too go in search of that one,
That eludes you and is just out of reach.
Maybe that's why you become a muse,
To the broken hearts!

Check out a video rendition of this poem here

Friendship Goals

Best paired with:
Woh Chand Khila, Woh Tare Hanse (Anari, 1959)

Maybe the moon
Laments about being lonely in the sky,
So the stars show up from time to time,
To give it some company.

Maybe the moon and stars
Disagree with each other on occasions,
So, there's only the moon or only the stars,
Visible in the sky sometimes.

Maybe the moon and stars
Venture out for adventures together,
So, the sky remains empty,
On some nights.

Maybe somebody behaves so intolerantly,
That others feel like kicking them out,
So, some stars stop showing up for a few days or
Have a falling out, which we get to witness as shooting stars.

Isn't that a friendship to get inspired from?
Maybe that should be our #FriendshipGoals from now on.

Scars to My Beautiful

Best paired with:
Chand Ko Daag Laga (Humara Watan, 1956)

What if?
Those spots we see on the moon,
aren't blemishes on its beauty.

What if?
The spots are
Nothing but scars,
Not unlike the scars we carry.

What if?
Like us,
The moon also got hurt,
And the spots are a mark of those hardships.

What if?
We could also learn to
Be beautiful and glowing,
Despite those scars.

What if?
Those scars could be
A badge of honour
A remembrance
A memoir
A test-in-time of our valour and strength
A star on our shoulders like a soldier.

What if?
We too can be identified
Beyond those spots.

What if?
Being scarred for life
With internal and external spots
To mark our bodies and minds
Could be not a blemish on our beauty,
But an add-on to our charms.

Check out a video rendition of this poem here

Shall We Count Stars Together?

Best paired with:
Taare Gin (Dil Bechara, 2020)

Gazing at the stars
Twinkling, shining, and glowing
In all their glorious beauty.

Some say it's for the dreamers,
An activity for those
A little off balance in their minds.

Dreaming takes courage though
And admiring beauty
Takes a keen eye,

Oblivion is a bliss
And forgetting about the world for a bit
We all deserve in once a while

Dear star gazers,
If you ever feel like it,
Shall we count stars together?

Avoiding the Crowd

Best paired with:
Chandra Re Chanda re (Sapnay, 1997)

If the Earth becomes uninhabitable
Or if it becomes possible to visit outer space
Without losing my mind or a few body parts
I would want to avoid humans or any crowd
Because they've already ruined one living space
So any planet is out of my list

Because men, they say
Are from Mars
And women,
From Venus

Hence, if I could, I would go to the Moon instead
We've known each other a long time anyway
It knows my secrets more than any living being
What with my late-night pondering and confessions
That little blob of white is my buddy!
My literal long-distance friend

And how wonderful would it be
To see, feel, and be atop something
I've been admiring and falling in love with a little more,
Every time I gaze at it

I'd be happily dedicating the lines from one of my favorite Bollywood songs
'आई ऐसी रात है जो
बहुत खुशनसीब है
चाहे जिसे दूर से दुनिया
वो मेरे करीब है'

Rough translation: Here comes a night that's very fortunate indeed. The one that the whole world loves from afar, is right next to me

Nightly Interlude

Poetry form: Tanka
Best paired with:
Saawli Si Raat (Barfi, 2012)

Day and its brightness
Overrated, tedious
Shining in darkness
Moon and twinkling friends, the stars
Sensuous, nighttime interlude

The Brightest Star

>Best paired with:
>*Chand Mera Dil (Hum Kisise Kum Naheen, 1977)*

You're like a guiding hand
To the dark side
of my world

You're the moonlight
And I'm the moon beams

You're the lone star in the dark sky
On a moonless night
Leading me to a brightness
I wouldn't have discovered otherwise

Quietude

Poetry form: Nonet
Best paired with:
Ye Raaten Nayi Puraani (Julie, 1975)

The opposite of chaos and noise
Darkness mostly carries some poise
It holds lot of secrets & joys
Silence enables ploys
The quietude employs
Most all enjoys
Some noise
Nice

Owl

Poetry form: Gogyohka
Best paired with:
Little Bird (Annie Lennox from Diva, 1992)

Creature of the night
Awake when the world sleeps
Hooting and unblinking
Maybe keeping watch
Is it also struggling to find peace?

Meteor

Poetry form: *Dizain*
Best paired with:
Shooting Stars (Monster High, 2015)

In a dark blanket of glittering stars
A disruptor warps the flawless vision
In a way maybe these too are memoirs
Knowledgeable ones call it, collision
Romantics for their wishes, provision
Such an enchanting sight, the sky shower
Maybe it's nature's attempt at a scour
Or a tiff with other celestial
The falling is a responsive glower
For the onlookers a nightfall special

Jasmine

Poetry form: Deibide Baise Fri Toin
Best paired with:
Raat Rani (Modern Love, 2022)

Alluring,
Its scent, all senses mooring
Can whiff only when it's dark
Lark

A delight
Rightly called Queen of the night
Green, white, or yellow, hue one
Stun

Nightfall
Its aroma makes a thrall
Lightless hour feat not to miss
This

Ghost

Poetry form: Cyhydedd Naw Ban
Best paired with:
Bhoot Hoon Mein (Bhoot, 2003)

Everyone's bit afraid of the dark
Shadows, silhouettes, and veiled motions
Echoes, chimes, heightened emotions
Owls hoot, cats meow, crickets chirp, dogs bark
The sounds and sights, signs of a mission
Show time for ghosts and apparitions

Heaven and Earth

Best paired with:
Yoon Shabnami (Saawariya, 2007)

How you tease us like this
Not showing up when we crave your sight the most
It's not fair on your part
To make your admirers wait such

But then it's okay I guess
Because in doing such a peek a boo
You teach us
Patience
And...
Not being available at the drop of a hat whenever someone calls for us
As then they'd take one for granted

Dear Eid and Karwa Chauth ka chand
You're just as wise as you're beautiful
One full, one less than half
Yet fulfilling similar tasks for the onlookers

You enlighten both literally and intrinsically
Being there matters
Showing up is important
Even when you're late
Even if your presence is not a hundred percent

Stay heavenly (see what I did there?)

From,
Your earthly aficionado

Readalong

Best paired with:
The Book I Read (Talking Heads, 1977)

One more page
Just another chapter
Oh! But how can I stop now?
I need to know what happens next.
Oh my God! I did not see that coming
Huh? Is it over?
Sigh!
Time to close it

Oh! Hey there…
Did you like it too?
Thanks for being there
You're my favourite readalong buddy
Even though you never seem to participate or respond
Okay! I'm going to sleep now, good night

Lamp off
Darkness engulf
The book outside continues to shine and twinkle
The black blanket with its millions illuminations and one white bubble
The one with a never-ending story

Midas Touch

Best paired with:
The Sky is My Canvas (Gui Gui Sui Sui, 2015)

The writer ran out of ink
The artist's stock of paint, exhausted
The midnight oil burned still
The creative minds left to fend without their tools

Gazing at the moon and stars
The writer saw his favourite notebook
The artist, his favourite canvas

Moon became the page and easel
Its friends, the stars
Pen to one, paintbrush to the other

Thus unfurled a story that would truly be
Written in the stars

Paparazzi

Best paired with:
I'll Be Thunder (Tina Turner, 1986)

Boom
Clap
Crack

And then…

A streak across the black
Silvery, shining,
Lighting up
Just for a few seconds

Nature's paparazzi is here
Smile!

At the End of the Day

Best paired with:
Sooraj Dooba Hain (Roy, 2015)

When the birds fly back to the their nests in flocks
When the sky turns into nature's colourful canvas
When I can stretch my arms and legs while sighing and shutting down the computer

When I gaze out the window soaking in the hues of the setting sun
When I sip on my favorite beverage and reflect on today and look forward to tomorrow

That's my favourite part of the day
Because I'm done with the tough and hopefully the worst part
Now it's time to relax
And indulge in guilty pleasures

They call it sundown, dusk, twilight
They call it the after or dark hours
For me, it's end of the day
And beginning of my happy hours
Before calling it a day

Secured

> Best paired with:
> *Chanda Ko Dhundne Sabhi Taare Nikal Pade (Jeene Ki Raah, 1969)*

Before humans discovered fire
Before sapiens invented electricity
Before earthlings understood and adapted to the world as they see it today
Before the populace began to feel unsafe despite all the Avant Garde gadgets at their disposal

They did it all
They do it today as well
And they'll keep at it for long after we're gone
It's not without reason we say
The stars will guide you home

Coupled with their big, white and blemished friend
These twinkling little ones
The ones we call
The moon and stars
Have been guarding the world and its treasures
In the darkness of night
Through their light

Community

Best paired with:
Sun and Moon and Stars (Anita Lester, 2021)
Or
Yeh Taara Woh Taara (Swades, 2004)

These twinkling forms in the sky at night
The ones named like animals, signs and what not

These shapes in the sky at night
Forming clusters and cconstellations

These glowing figures in the sky at night
Forming a community and a closed group of sorts

These celestial bodies in the sky at night
Are they a replica, a model of sorts about the human existence
Or is the other way round?

Lapping it Up

> Best paired with:
> *Raat Bhi Hai Kuch Bheegi Bheegi (Mujhe Jeene Do, 1963)*

People die on your watch, there's also new life
People mourn in your lap, there's also the feeling of bliss
People sleep in your embrace, there's also insomnia
People reminisce in your presence, there's also creation of new memories

They call you the dark hours
Maybe they should call you grey
You're neither black nor white,
And definitely not colourful

But there's a sense of comfort
A known familiarity
Sometimes bad, mostly good

Like a mother's lap
Like a friend's shoulder
Like a favourite quilt
Where we find peace
Where we find a safe-space
Where we eventually fall asleep
Against all odds
Despite our erratic moods

The Light at the End of the Tunnel

Best paired with:
Raat Bhar Ka Mehmaan Andhera (Sone Ki Chidiya, 1958)

This tunnel
It's endless
It's dark
It's scary
It's unforgiving
It has some lights, shining, twinkling
Just enough
To give strength
To give hope
To make you believe it's temporary

Because
There's light at the end
Such that
It'll swallow the darkness
It'll keep you going for a while
It'll make you forget what you left behind
Just long enough
To give strength
To brave up
To make you understand
There's another tunnel coming up again
And there's no escaping this phenomena of light and dark

Cry Wolf

Best paired with:
Wolf Moon (Type O Negative, 1996)
Or
Jungle Mein Kaand (Bhediya, 2022)

It's a beautiful, romanticized and eagerly awaited sight
For most

There are sighs, moans, epiphanies, life-learnings in its presence
For most

Turning over a new leaf, letting go of guilt and mistakes
For most

But…

It's a horrifying, agonizing and distressed arrival
For a few

There's howling, crying, cursing one's existence in its presence
For a few

Turning into a monster, becoming someone hateful
For a few

The full moon
Means something to everyone
Be it for most
Be it for a few

Not Alone

> Best paired with:
> *Chaandni Raatein (Shamsa Kanwal, 1996)*

Oh!
My dearest friend, I've been awaiting you
Let me tell you what's new

Oh!
My closest buddy, you're there on most days
You listen patiently to everything I say

Oh!
My faithful companion, your light streaming in through the window and curtain
Turns my loneliness into solitude for a period certain

Oh!
My best pal, you show up more than anyone
Can you promise not to break my heart like most others have done?

Pursuits

Routine

Poetry form: Cascade

Best paired with:

Naadan Parindey (Rockstar, 2011)

A routine day
Hustling, shuffling, constantly doing something
Mostly the same, rarely anything new
Where's the excitement?

Sunrise to sunset
Morning to night
That's where it ends
A routine day

The sky changes color, and birds bound home as you too return to your haven
The lights come on and then turn off
Within it all, you forget for a while
Hustling, shuffling, constantly doing something

Meet, chat, smile
Different in the PM than AM
Things and activities done then, don't feel like
Mostly the same, rarely anything new

Clock chimes
Alarm blares
Another day, but also another night, move on, don't wonder
Where's the excitement?

An Insomniac's Plight

Best paired with:
So Gaya Yeh Jahaan (Tezaab, 1988)

Sleep ditching again
Thoughts invading relentless
The world dreams and rests
The insomniac ponders on
Life, unfairness, mysteries

Bonfire

Poetry form: Anaphora
Best paired with:
Sham (Aisha, 2010)

Don't put this fire out
It's beautiful like some
But not menacing, unlike most

Don't put this fire out
It's giving warmth
To the body and the soul

Don't put this fire out
It's creating memories
With friends, family, and strangers alike

Don't put this fire out
It's unveiling candid thoughts and long-forgotten memoirs
Leading to heart-to-heart, deep conversations

Don't put this fire out
It's letting guitar chords, harmonica tunes, and the chorus humming
Mingle with the sounds of nature

Don't put this fire out,
It's letting people soak in
The beauty of Mother Earth engulfs them

Don't put this fire out,
It's helping those around it
Forget their routines and woes

Don't put this fire out,
For as long as it burns
There'll be more smiles and fewer frowns

Don't put this fire out,
Its embers a souvenir
The minutes, a keepsake

Taken for a Ride

Poetry form: The Bop
Best paired with:
Helter Skelter (The Beatles, 1968)

Small, medium, and large
Rides of all sizes, for people of every age
Some going up and down, some moving in circles
All illuminated and brightly lit
The lights inviting me toward them
Their haphazard movements making me skeptical

My first time at a carnival was fun and fearful

The Ferris wheel, the roller coaster, the pendulum ride,
The carousel, the bumping cars, the swing ride
I tried most, I skipped some
The scaredy cat in me won sometimes
Other times, it was the thriller seeker
As the rides would start, crying out of terror, then exhilaration
The view from the top, the tiny dots of scattered lights
Made it all worth fighting off the trepidation

My first time at a carnival was fun and fearful

The disappointment of missing out on the most forbidding rides,
Compensated by the yummy food and the plethora of shopping
But most of all, by the adventure at the Valley of Death
And the fun inside the Mirror Maze
I ate till my stomach hurt, purchased everything my heart desired
It would be a night I'll remember for long

My first time at a carnival was fun and fearful

Dream or Goal?

Poetry form: Bref double

Best paired with:

Zindagi Khwaab Hai (Jaagte Raho, 1956)

A different world
A better billet
Nothing is impossible here
It's a magical place

No barriers or limits
More smiles, fewer tears
Eyes remain closed
Every other sense with pleasure laced

People we care for, places we love
All there, everything scintillates
Bad things forgotten, the good multiplied
You can even bid goodbye to the rat race

It's not a reality, but it can be
If with eyes open, we call it our ***goal*** and work towards its chase

Burning the Effigy

Poetry form: Clerihew

Best paired with:
Raavan (Songs of Trance, 2020)

Dasagriva Lankapati Ravan
was nothing short of a maven
Every year I saw him burning
The experience a learning, somewhat discerning, a bit concerning

Fireworks

Poetry form: Cyhydedd Fer Poems
Best paired with:
Firework (Teenage Dream, 2010)

Boom, bang, blast, burst, flash, whoosh, whistle
Crackling sounds, flashing lights, bristle

Illuminations, dazzling
A jubilation, raveling

Celebration, sight to behold
Onlookers attentions ahold

Sky, a gamut of lit-up shades
Fountains, sparkles, rockets, cascade

Zapper

Poetry form: Con-Verse

Best paired with:

Flea Fly Mosquito (The Kiboomers, 2013)

Looks like something you play with
But that's not what you should doeth

It's nothing short of a saviour
Protecting from bugs behaviour

In the dark, it provides much respite
From creatures keeping us up all night

Signs

Poetry form: Brevette
Best paired with:
The Yawn Song (Marky Monday, 2019)

Mouth
o p e n s
fatigue

Xanax

Poetry form: Octameter
Best paired with:
Udd gaye (Ritviz, 2019)

Easy escape route
Pop one or two in
Time to say goodbye
Ciao anxiety
Hello there dreamland
Smiles, notoriety
No frowns or sorrow
Giggles, Gaiety

Happiness galore
Forget fears and doubts
You can jump, run, fly
Have worries no more
Friends or solo, fun
Go beyond the shore
No society
Just variety

Disclaimer: Xanax is a prescription pill/drug and should not be consumed as a recreational drug without proper medical advice or opinion. Consuming it without doing so could be hazardous for health and can lead to long-term ill/side effects on the body and mind.

a(W)ake

Poetry form: Musette
Best paired with:
Chanda Ki Bindiyaa (Mai, 2013)

No sleep
Up yet again
Sigh deep

Toss, turn
Eyes keep staring
Rest yearn

Thoughts stir
Mind, body, rest
Confer

Calm, hush
The outside dark
Sleep shush

Un(V)eil

Poetry form: Lento
Best paired with:
Parde Mein Rehne Do (Shikar, 1968)

Grace hidden in the layers
Trace of what's inside, implored
Chase futile during the brightness of day
Face and figure, in the darkness of night, exposed

Veiled and secretive so far
Flailed to reveal it whole
Exhaled in anticipation of what lays beneath
Unveiled, blushing face and eyes rimmed with kohl

Union

Poetry form: Etheree

Best paired with:

Tere Mere Milan Ki Yeh Raina (Abhimaan, 1973)

Tonight's going to be memorable
He had planned it all for a long time
The mood, the setting, and the food
The ambiance was perfect too
Their favourite movie
Followed by music
Somas closing
Hearts connect
Union
First

New
For both
Encounter
Unlike before
Only mind and soul
Emotional connect
This affinity beyond
Words, conversations, sweet nothings
She knows what it means and wants it too
Little shy but ready to take the plunge

Poetry form: Etheree

Tenting

Poetry form: Ballad
Best paired with:
Night Sky (Faime, 2022)

Not home
But a happy place
For some hours or days
Adventure's base

Small and cozy
Limited in its space
Sleeping in its arms
With nature, a chase

Going back to our roots
Slows down life's pace
Fun in going back to basics
Losing sense of time and space

Not home
But a happy place
For some hours or days
Adventure's base

Stay alone or with family and friends,
A great way to forget routine ruts and race
Observe the sky, stars, and the moon
As their lights seep through the abode's lace

Trees, birds, animals, insects
Each other's steps you trace
They provide you company
While at the blanket of celestials, you gaze

Not home
But a happy place

For some hours or days
Adventure's base

Stargazing

Poetry form: Acrostic
Best paired with:
Tim Tim Taaron Ke Deep Jale (Mausi, 1958)

S – Sleepless night's pursuit

T – Turning frowns into smiles

A – Allows minds to wonder and stare in amazement, even answering some questions

R – Relaxes one and all, irrespective of gender and ages

G – Gazing, pondering, marvelling

A – At the grey, black, dark blue, sky

Z – Zenith of sparkles, twinkles; luminous and glittering

I – In the open, from the rooftop, or peeking through curtains and windows

N – Night made alluring

G – (by) Gem-like celestial things

Rooftop

Poetry form: Triolet

Best paired with:
Chand Chupa Badal Mein (Hum Dil De Chuke Sanam, 1999)

Stars twinkle a little brighter tonight
Are you also thinking about that time?
From up above, we saw world, small yet bright
Stars twinkle a little brighter tonight
Nothing scared us, neither dark nor the height
I often wonder how we made that climb
Stars twinkle a little brighter tonight
Are you also thinking about that time?

Pajamas

Poetry form: Echo Verse
Best paired with:
Pajama Time!(Laurie Berkner, 2016)

They guarantee a good nap
Nap!
The comfort they provide is matched by no other cloth
Cloth!
Cotton, flannel, linen, fleece, or silk
Silk!
Full, half, capris, or shorts
Shorts!
Adorned with bunnies, kitties, dogs, pandas, or cats
Cats!
They're with what, we call it a day
Day!
Ironically something we only wear at night
Night!
But given a choice, we'd keep them on all the time
Time!

Nightclub

Poetry form: Endecha
Best paired with:
Dance Basanti(Ungli,2014)

It's time to start the party
On the music, Off the lights
Baby sway, twirl, spin, and whirl
Let go of all the fears from your mind and sights

Your favourite song came on
Oh, baby what more you want?
This is the chance, rock and dance
For once, darling you can let go of that daunt

Dark but not scarily so
A blending of hide and show
Step up, step down, break a leg
Your face honey shines amidst scintillating glow

Move to tunes, match rhythm
This place, the nightclub, a mood
They call these the sinful hours
But sweetheart, you don't need to, about that brood

Lovemaking

Poetry form: Descort
Best paired with:
Lag Jaa Gale (Woh Kaun Thi, 1964)
Or
Zara Zara (Rehna Hai Tere Dil Mein, 2001)

Eyes clashed
A pair of browns with a pair of greens
Instant appraising, resulting in appreciation from both sides
The message communicated and conveyed
Two people at a bar found what they were looking for

Drinks turned to dinner
Which became a first date, a good one for both
Followed by a few more
Till things got to a point where one of them asked
"Would you like to come up for coffee?"

None missed the innuendo
Neither denied the body's wanting
A fervent, "Yes" from the other's mouth
A night full of passion followed

Lips on lips
Bodies touching
All inhibitions were forgotten
Clothes discarded, like a hindrance in their meeting

The beverage offered was enjoyed later
Brewing conversations after an arduous lovemaking
No promises exchanged, and no future plans were laid
It was a night unlike most, for them, it would remain the first of many

Call it A Night

Poetry form: Wrapped Refrain

Best paired with:

Chal Lade Re Bhaiya (Revolver Rani, 2014)

Call it a night, time to bid bye
Mouth opened and escaped a sigh
Of tiredness, fatigue, a sign
Mind, body, draws a limit line
Eyes drooping and shutting, to stay open they fight
Tuck into dreamland and sleep well…Call it a night

Tuck into fantasm, forget world
In comforter cozily curled
You've sweated and worked hard all-day
Time to let the mind go astray
With that yawn, your mouth opens wide, much like a chasm
Shut out lights, all else aside…Tuck into fantasm

Karaoke

Poetic form: Diminishing verse

Best paired with:
Too Drunk to Karaoke (Toby Keith and Jimmy Buffett, 2013)

They said it would be amusing
I gave it a little musing
Not averse to new experiences and things using
After all, it'd only be some minutes or few hours of songs to sing

The event took place not much outside the work estate
Everyone was in a different, jovial state
Some participated big, some nil, and most a tate
The food and drinks though everyone heartily drank and ate

It became a night to remember
Some booked online in advance as an e-member
Late deciders booked on-the-spot and joined as an offline member
The moments, laughter and smiles, will forever remain an ember

Insomnia

Poetry form: Decima
Best paired with:
Fireflies (Ocean Eyes, 2009)

Tossing, turning, rolling about
Overwhelming, restless feeling
Nasty thoughts, events, peace stealing
The mind wishes for a blackout
From this known but unpleasant route
What will it take for comatose
It doesn't come even with eyes close
The body tired, so is the mind
Dear sleep, just be a little kind?
And give tonight, a little dose?

Hunger

Poetry form: Dansa
Best paired with:
What's Going On (Salaam Namaste, 2005)

What's this odd-hour craving
I want all kinds of food
Such is the mood
Tummy weirdly behaving
What's this odd-hour craving

Refrigerator and pantry I intrude
Snacks hogged, appetite a bit I subdue
Leftovers from the day, life-saving
What's this odd-hour craving

Munchies devoured, coffee brewed
The midnight adventures finally conclude
It comes every once in a while, waving
This odd-hour craving

Do it All Tonight

Poetic form: Lyrical

Best paired with:

Kudi Nu Nachne De (Angrezi Medium, 2020)

Hit it, hit it, baby
Hit your feet on the floor
And get your body moving as you sing along
With your favorite song, this is where you belong

Pull it, pull it, baby
Pull the quilt around yourself
And get your body comfortable in that favorite chair
Let the words wash over you as you read without a care

Relax, relax, baby
Lie down in the warm bath water with some candles around
Let the lather soothe you as you read and drink
You deserve that self-love more than you think

Gobble, Gobble, baby
Relish the dish you craved and maybe pair it up with a favorite beverage
Let its deliciousness satisfy thou
Good food is all you need for now

Plomp, plomp, baby
Sit yourself at that window sill or balcony
Take in the city's skyline view
Watch the juxtaposition of its calmness and bustle, surprise you anew

Pick up, pick up, baby
Pick up the phone and call or text those you've been meaning to
Ask if they're fine and what they're up to
Reminisce the good times for minutes few

Click, click, baby
Click away on the keyboard and pour out all your feelings
Let the city, music, and food, inspire you
To write out the piece you've been meaning to get through

Kiss, Kiss, baby
Kiss the one you're lucky to have by your side
Maybe watch a movie or go out for a drive
Hold their hand and tell them you love them as the night comes alive

Do it, do it, baby
Do it all tonight
It's all about the now and here
Who knows when another time is near?

Ouija

Poetic form: Terza Rima Sonnet

Best paired with:

Thriller (Michael Jackson, 1982)

Bored, why not call upon a spirit for fun
Bring out the board, think of a dead person's name
He or she doesn't matter, be strong and fear none

With all things in place, time to begin the game
Do you hear us, can you answer our queries
Are you in the house, can you confirm and claim?

Fingers on the board move slowly in series
Wind howls, footsteps echo and windows rattle
Summoners nervously confirm theories

Between the living and the dead, a battle
Excitement and novelty soon turned to fright
Worry mounting on how to end or settle

It turned out to be a long-enduring night
Everyone involved was never quite alright

Burning the Midnight Oil

> Best paired with:
> *Aaj Ki Raat (Don-The Chase Begins Again, 2006)*

Even if it feels like
You're tired
You've got to go on

Even if it feels like
It's out of your understanding
You've got to at least try

Even if it feels like
You don't have enough time to do it all
You've got to finish as much as you can

Even if it feels like
You're gonna fail anyway
You've got to prep yourself so you can tell yourself you gave it your best

Even if it feels like
You've no idea why you're doing this
You've got to just look back and reflect on what brought you here

Even if it feels like
You're the only one up at this ungodly hour
You've got to just look up and out of the window to notice at least one other light on too

Even if it feels like
You're alone or lonely
You've got to find peace and solace in that beacon of light giving you hope that there's someone else in this boat too

Preparing for the Morrow

Best paired with:
Gonna Fly Now (Rocky, 1976)

Stay up,
It's not yet time to call it a night

Stay up,
You've to let go of everything that's happened today and before that

Stay up,
You've to look back, analyse your work for the day and be grateful for it all

Stay up,
You've to say goodbye to the day gone by

Stay up,
You've to make plans for the coming day

Stay up,
You've to turn it all off, the TV, the phone, the Wi-Fi, and your mind

Stay up,
You've to be prepared for what's to come

Stay up,
You've to show up better than yesterday

Let's Make Tonight Special

Best paired with:
Aye Udi Udi (Saathiya, 2002)

Oh, Baby!
We haven't done this before
Why don't we give it a go?
Hold my hand, and forget it all
Let's you and I go on a date

Oh, Baby!
We haven't admired each other before
Why not dress up a bit?
Wear what our hearts always desired
Let's you and I be beautiful together

Oh, Baby!
We haven't had the chance before
Why not now?
Tell me your favourite movie
Let's you and I watch it together

Oh, Baby!
We haven't talked much before
Why not go out for dinner?
Tell me about your day, I'll tell you about mine
Let's you and I open up our hearts

Oh, Baby!
We haven't been alone before
Why not have some privacy?
Make it possible for our bodies to explore and touch our most intimate parts
Let's you and I, make it special tonight

Check out a video rendition of this poem here

A Dark Winter Night

Best paired with:
Dekho Na (Fanaa, 2006)

'twas a dark, winter night
The forecast indicating it was the coldest of the season by far
Then the snow showed up
Making the gloom worse, or maybe better

'twas a sight both dull and cheerful
The lights and décor indicating the festive season was near
Then you showed up
Making my night joyful, or maybe a tragedy

'twas a time we'll both remember
The car in my front yard indicating a flat tyre
Then my hospitable side showed up
Making my house bustle, or maybe a bit too noisy

'twas a sad and awkward first encounter
The grumbling stomachs indicating hungry individuals
Then my intuitive side showed up
Making the dining room our date, or maybe a first of many

'twas a bit better after that
The conversation flowed easily indicating growing affinity
Then my dormant outgoing side showed up
Making the best of ourselves reveal itself, or maybe saving the worse for later

'twas a movie date after that
The snow storm outside indicating the need to cuddle for warmth
Then our passionate sides showed up
Making the next step obvious, or maybe meant-to-be

'twas a whirlwind affair after that
The relationship grew strong indicating stability

Then our worse showed up
Making the days a bit sour, or maybe turning the night extra *lascivious*

'twas a long and stressful journey forward
The nights turned from cold to warm indicating change of season
Then our tolerant sides showed up
Making our journey together acceptable, or maybe heading towards rebuff

'twas a pleasant, windy night
The full moon and twinkling stars indicating a chance to rekindle our romance
Then neither you nor your car showed up
Making my heart break, or maybe making it resolute to not give up

'twas a dark, winter night
The forecast indicating it was the coldest of the season by far
Then the snow showed up
Making my gloom worse, or maybe the hope stronger

'twas a sight both dull and cheerful
The lights and décor indicating the festive season was near
Then you showed up
Making us recall where it all began, or maybe why we were here

The Force

Best paired with:
Ye Sham Mastani (Kati Patang, 1971)

That was the night
I remember
Our gaze clashing
My breath hitching
My heart beating
A sight for the sore eyes
Her face
A beguiling force

That was the night
I remember
Our conversation flowing
My lips smiling
My mind relaxing
A balm for the lonely soul
Her camaraderie
A soothing force

That was the night
I remember
Our memories in-making
My moments filling
My happiness manifolding
A remedy for the answers I was seeking
Her hold
A promising force

That was the night
I remember
Our silent understanding
My words failing
My feelings faltering
A compassionate listener to my vulnerability

Her embrace
A reassuring force

That was the night
I remember
Our hands and feet touching
My skin tingling
My senses titillating
A quench for the thirsty bod
Her scrutiny
A raging force

That was the night
I remember
Our relationship beginning
My life changing
My hopes fulfilling
A plus one for my negating persona
Her acceptance
A never-ending force

For A Spin

Best paired with:
Yun Hi Chala Chal (Swades,2004)

It's all hushed
It's all unrushed
Now is the right time
Let's take the car out
Take it for a spin

We have companions with us
We have everything thus
Now is the right time
Let's do what the heart desires
Take a tour of the place we live in

The city is still
The traffic is nil
Now is the right time
Let's roll the windows down
Take the fresh air in

There's no one around
There's no one to bound
Now is the right time
Let's play the music we love
Take in the lyrics and its meaning

The roads are deserted
The minds are diverted
Now is the right time
Let's sing along loud
Take the opportunity and be free with our kin

The view, unhindered
The sky, un-hazed
Now is the right time

Let's look up
Take time to admire moon's glow and stars twinkling

Did That Happen

Best paired with:
Manali Trance (The Shaukeens, 2014)

Puffs
Drags
Coughs
Sighs
We passed it around
And felt united in our woes

Some here
Some there
Some full
Some shared
We rolled and lit for others some
And some we got rolled and lit by others

The walls
The trees
The moon
The stars
We talked to them
And they talked back

Life's mysteries
Life's purpose
Life's unfairness
Life's meaning
We questioned
And we got the answers

Did we imagine it
Did it happen
Did we become high
Did we kill our lows
We were talking about senseless things
And somehow we still made sense though

NiSA Playlist

Song List
Chand Bhi Koi Deewana Hai (Apna Ghar Apni Kahaani, 1968)
Woh Chand Khila Woh Taare Hanse (Anari, 1959)
Chand Ko Daag Laga (Humara Watan, 1956)
Taare Gin (Dil Bechara, 2020)
Chanda Re Chanda Re (Sapnay, 1997)
Saawli Si Raat (Barfi!, 2012)
Chand Mera Dil (Hum Kisise Kum Naheen, 1977)
Ye Raat Nayi Puraani (Julie, 1975)
Little Bird (Anne Lennox from Diva, 1992)
Shooting Stars (Monster High, 2015)
Raat Raani (Modern Love, 2022)
Bhoot Hoon Mein (Bhoot, 2003)
Yoon Shabnami (Saawariya, 2007)
The Book I Read (Talking Heads, 1977)
The Sky is My Canvas (Gui Gui Sui Sui, 2015)
I'll Be Thunder (Tina Turner, 1986)
Sooraj Dooba Hain (Roy, 2015)

Chand ko Dhoodne Sabhi Taare Nikal Pade (Jeene Ki Raah, 1969)
Sun and Moon and Stars (Anita Lester, 2021)
Yeh Taara Woh Taara (Swades, 2004)
Raat Bhi Hai Kuch Bheegi Bheegi (Mujhe Jeene Do, 1963)
Raat Bhar Ka Mehmaan Andhera (Sone Ki Chidiya, 1958)
Wolf Moon (Type O Negative, 1996)
Jungle Mein Kaand (Bhediya, 2022)
Chaandni Raatein (Shamsa Kanwal, 1996)
Naadan Parindey (Rockstar, 2011)
So Gaya Yeh Jahaan (Tezaab, 1988)
Sham (Aisha, 2010)
Helter Skelter (The Beatles, 1968)
Zindagi Khwaab Hai (Jaagte Raho, 1956)
Raavan (Songs of Trance, 2020)
Firework (Teenage Dream, 2010)
Flea Fly Mosquito (The Kiboomers, 2013)
The Yawn Song (Marky Monday, 2019)
Udd Gaye (Ritviz, 2019)
Chanda Ki Bindiyaa (Mai, 2013)
Parde Mein Rehne Do (Shikhar, 1968)

Tere Mere Milan Ki Ye Raina (Abhimaan, 1973)
Night Sky (Faime, 2022)
Tim Tim Taaron Ke Deep Jale (Mausi, 1958)
Chand Chupa Badal Mein (Hum Dil, De Chuke Sanam, 1999)
Pajama Time! (Laurie Berkner, 2016)
Dance Basanti (Ungli, 2014)
Lag Jaa Gale (Woh Kaun Thi, 1964)
Zara Zara (Rehna Hai Tere Dil Mein, 2001)
Chal Lade Re Bhaiya (Revolver Rani, 2014)
Too Drunk to Karaoke (Toby Keith and Jimmy Buffett, 2013)
Fireflies (Ocean Eyes, 2009)
What's Going On (Salaam Namaste, 2005)
Kudi Nu Nachne De (Angrezi Medium, 2020)
Thriller (Michael Jackson, 1982)
Aaj Ki Raat (Don-The Chase Begins Again, 2006)
Gonna Fly Now (Rocky, 1976)
Aye Udi Udi (Saathiya, 2002)
Dekho Na (Fanaa, 2006)
Ye Sham Mastani (Kati Patang, 1971)
Manali Trance (The Shaukeens, 2014)
Yun Hi Chala Chal (Swades, 2004)

Listen to the songs on YouTube and Amazon Music

(Note: All the songs from the above playlist are available only on the YouTube playlist of NiSA because Amazon Music does not have some of the songs in its library)

Other Books by This Author

Love (Try) Angle (Love Trials I)

Ayesha has just moved to the 'City of Dreams' with her parents. She befriends the charming Viren, who helps her find her footing in Mumbai. Though she is slowly adjusting to her new life, what Ayesha is most excited about is pursuing B.A. (Hons.) Political Science from a reputed college. Things don't go as smoothly as she had thought though. Because Abhi, her senior, seems hell-bent on making her life on the campus difficult from day one. Just when things seem settled, Viren joins the college as an Ad-Hoc lecturer. Is there more to Ayesha's friendship with Viren, and her frenemity with Abhi? It seems there's a love triangle blooming around the corner or will it be a Love (Try) Angle? Because Ayesha is not sure if it's love at all.

Love & (Mellow) Drama - Love Trials II

Gayatri Kulkarni: A Gen-Z girl who has always lived under the shadow of her elder brother Sharad; so much so that she even chose her degree and college following in his footsteps. Although she doesn't regret it, she wishes her parents would understand her dream to pursue her one true passion - DANCE.
Varun Agarwal: A millennial who believes there are no shortcuts in life. He has learned the hard way that being born into a wealthy family comes with more cons than the world would ever understand.
She belongs to a Maharashtrian middle-class family from the suburbs. He hails from an affluent family in South Bombay. The only common point between them - being Mumbaikars. How do their paths cross in this city of dreams? Gayatri believes it's because of Abhi Agarwal, Varun's younger brother, who also happens to be her brother's batchmate and close friend. But Varun has harboured a crush on her long before they exchanged hellos and phone numbers.
Their story is a meeting of two generations and families, who are poles

apart. Is there drama involved? Gayatri is often called a drama queen by those who know her. But after Varun's entry into her life, she's transformed from Miss Melodrama to Miss Mellowed Drama. Find out all about that transition in this much-awaited spin-off from Manali Desai's debut novel, **Love (Try) Angle**, **Love & (Mellow) Drama (Love Trials-II)**

Mindful Musings & Peaceful Ponderings

Anxious

Conflicted

Nervous

Confused

Safe

Complete

Jubilant

Confident

Do these sound familiar? You may not have experienced these *feelings* lately or maybe not at all. But if you have, you aren't alone. The 50 poems in this book are a reflection of you, me, and all of us. They are the mindful musings and peaceful ponderings of human experiences that make us smile, laugh, cry, and wonder with emotions, that unite us all.

Under the Mistletoe & Other Stories

Diana is all set to welcome her loved ones for Christmas. An unexpected (and uninvited!) guest shows up at her door, spoiling her festive mood. All her attempts to thwart Dylan's intrusion go in vain as he keeps dropping in, again and again, insisting that she join his family for Christmas Eve dinner. Against her better judgment, she finally gives in, just to get him off her back. As they stand under the mistletoe after the dinner, Diana and Dylan know things have changed for the better for both.

A group of passengers is stranded at the airport together on New Year's Eve. Their plans were to celebrate the last day of the year and then ring in the new year with their loved ones by their side. But a delayed flight mars their plans and their happiness. They end up talking to each other, exchanging their New Year's Eve plans and how they celebrated it these many years so far. As they all welcome the new year together at midnight, their combined resolutions are to stay in touch with each other. They also resolve to make the best out of whatever life throws their way. Because as they have seen and experienced, not all things go as planned, always.

Samantha is visiting her native, Benakatti, after many years. Even though it's Christmas time, it's not a happy occasion in the family. As friends and family drop in for a visit, Samantha recalls the many winter breaks she spent in this village as a child. An unexpected guest shows up one day, bringing forth a cherished memory they had made on a foggy winter day many years ago.

These and 10 other stories encompass this festive special anthology. These are stories of hope, love, healing, new beginnings, acceptance, and everything that the holidays represent.

The Art of Being Grateful & Other Stories

Aashna receives a mysterious phone call in the middle of the night. The caller is a girl who says she has been kidnapped and will die if Aashna doesn't help her. Before Aashna can get details about the girl and her whereabouts, the phone gets cut off. Who was she and why did her voice sound eerily familiar? Will Aashna be able to help her?

Maanvi's life has always been about making everyone around realize that she is worthy too. From her test grades to her body type, everyone always had a piece of advice to give or some judgement to pass. How does Maanvi get affected by these? Does she manage to prove her worth to the world?

These and six other stories in this collection, cover a range of genres including romance, mystery, horror, thriller and much more. Delve in for a delightful reading journey!

The Untold Stories

Have you wondered about the events that happen around us? Do you think about the kind of lives people we come across everyday lead, and how they came to be what they are today? Our life is our story, but what about those little everyday incidents which create the anecdotes filling up the chapters of our life story? 'The Untold Stories' shares tiny anecdotes from people's everyday routines which go on to make remarkable chapters in their life stories. These anecdotes range from incidents around contemporary social issues and events such as terrorism and environmental imbalance to those circling around relationships.

A Rustic Mind

"We never think about the effects or repercussions of our everyday actions or even the things we come across on daily basis. Through 'A Rustic Mind' I aim to provide a thoughtful take on such actions and incidents. Poetic in its expression, these words will strike a chord which is not only deep but relatable on many levels. "

Ten Tales

This is a collection of short stories by authors across the world. The stories have been handpicked and selected based on their quality. The stories cover all genres in fiction.

Manali's story in this book is titled 'I'm Glad I'm Not Beautiful'. It spins a story around the much needed to be curbed issue and social stigma of acid attacks. The story circles around two school-going teenage girls, Abha and Vidhya, who are best friends, but are opposite in nature and appearance, and how a few incidents on a particular day turns their lives upside down.

Zista

"Zista represents Culture, the hub of which lies in India."

This title holds in its pages the very essence of India, its people and its culture, conveyed through a selection of short stories by few of the best authors of India.

Manali's story in this book is titled 'The Walls Have Ears'. This story helped her bag the Best Script Award. It talks about a young girl's day out in the infamous Kamathipura aka The Red-Light District of Mumbai.

Petrichor (compiled and edited by Manali Desai)

14 writers

7 short stories

9 poems

Who doesn't hold a special love for the rains? The smell of wet soil when the showers hit the surface of the Earth, opens up so much for us, emotionally. In this magical collection, we have some of the most special monsoon stories from a bunch of talented writers across the world. The contributors of this anthology traverse from 8 years old to 30 years old. What's common between them? Their love for monsoons of course! Because love for the rains is not age bound, right? This anthology is an attempt at bringing together writers from various walks of life. Each story or poem in this collection will make you rekindle your love with this most beloved season. It will be hard not to reminisce about your many romances with Indra over the years. The pages within this book will evoke nostalgic feelings in every reader. So, grab a cup of your favorite beverage and cozy up in your reading nook as you delve into Petrichor.

About the Author

Manali Desai

Manali is a full-time freelance writer and editor cum blogger. Currently, apart from her ad hoc writing and editing assignments, Manali runs a blog where she shares poetry, short fiction, book reviews, and personal stories. In her authoring journey, Manali has had nine books published under her name. Alongside that, she has also been a part of a few co-authored books (aka anthologies). Manali is a bestselling author on Amazon India with all her books ranking in the top ten in many categories. Her short story, *The Walls Have Ears*, helped her bag the Best Short Story Award in 2019 at *Stories from India* by Ukiyoto Publishing. She has also won the Best Author: Fiction Award at *Cherry Books Awards*, and the Book of The Year title in 2021 at *BeTales Magazine Annual Awards*, for her debut novel, **Love (Try) Angle**. Her short story titled, **The (Un)Blind Date**, which is a part of her Christmas special anthology, **Under the Mistletoe & Other Stories**, won the best story prize in an online contest by smitawritespen.com, before the book's release in December 2021. Her second novel, **Love & (Mellow) Drama,** was nominated for the prestigious *AutHER Awards* by Times of India in 2023. The same book also helped her win Best Author of the Year at *Authoropod Magazine Annual Awards '23*. You can find her on all socials as **A Rustic Mind**.

www.ingramcontent.com/pod-product-compliance
Lightning Source LLC
LaVergne TN
LVHW041540070526
838199LV00046B/1767